The Giggle Box

written by Patricia Schoch

illustrated by Lisa Lowell

The Giggle Box

First Edition
1 2 3 4 5 6 7 8 9 10

ISBN 978-1530107131

Printed in the USA

Dedicated

In loving memory of my beautiful and talented
mother, Thelma E. Kelchner, who passed along to me
her passion for writing, and in loving honor of my
wonderful husband, Denny, and our four beautiful
children, Christa, Bryan, David, and Adam - the
inspirations for my book and my life.

Davey is a happy little boy. Ever since he was very little, he loved to giggle.

He giggled in the morning when his puppy licked his toes.

He giggled at night when his Mommy made silly faces while she read books to him.

He giggled when his Daddy tried to wash his neck in the bathtub.

He giggled when his big sister, Christy, swung him around and made him dizzy.

He giggled when his big brother, Bryan, hit a sour note on his trumpet.

And, he giggled when his baby brother, Adam, put his pants on backwards. He was such a giggle box!

Now Davey goes to school and he still loves to giggle! Every day he excitedly climbs into the bus.

One day, everyone was laughing and talking so loudly that the bus driver yelled, "This bus is too noisy! Tomorrow I am going to change everyone's seat!"

The next day, Davey found himself sitting with a new boy named Michael. Davey didn't know him very well because Michael didn't talk much.

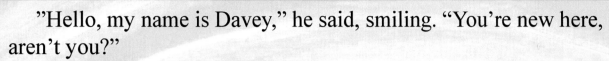

"Hello, my name is Davey," he said, smiling. "You're new here, aren't you?"

"Yes," replied Michael.

"Do you like baseball?" asked Davey.

"Sort of, but I'm not very good." Michael was quiet and didn't smile much, either.

Davey decided he wanted to help him make some friends.

Every day he would talk to Michael and try to make him laugh. "Hey, Michael! Look at that silly dog out there chasing his tail! I wonder if he really thinks he's going to catch it!"

And every day Michael would smile just a little and look out the window. Davey felt sad for Michael and wanted to help him feel better.

Now, somewhere up in Laughterland, which is where the fluffiest, most tickly clouds float, a happy fairy named Giggleina watched Davey try hard to make Michael laugh.

"I think Davey needs a little help down there," she thought.

That night, she went into her closet and got out her very special Giggle Box. Each night while all the little giggle boxes are sound asleep, Giggleina tiptoes into their rooms, collects a handful of their giggles and places them lovingly into her Giggle Box. When it is full, she flits back home to her very own special cloud in Laughterland. She carefully puts her Giggle Box back in the closet and goes to sleep, until she can find someone else who needs some giggles.

Giggleina is also very smart! She says, "Giggles are like flowers. As long as you pick them carefully, without pulling out the roots, they will grow more giggles. Giggles make people happy when they are shared, especially with someone who doesn't have many."

Tonight, she decided to help Davey share his wonderful gift of laughter with Michael.

After Davey was sound asleep, she quietly floated into his room, collected some giggles and placed them carefully into her box.

When it was full, she went to visit a sleeping Michael and sprinkled Davey's giggles all over him! Then, with a soft little giggle of her own, she disappeared.

The next morning, as usual, Davey sat next to Michael on the bus. "Look at those clouds up there. They look like frogs in pajamas," he said, giggling. Michael giggled, ever so slightly. Surprised, Davey giggled, again.

Michael giggled again, and Davey giggled again. Soon they were giggling so much that they didn't even know when the bus got to school! They even made the bus driver giggle, and she didn't get mad! Giggles can spread very fast!

Davey and Michael became great friends. They talked and laughed every day. Davey introduced Michael to his friends.

"Hey, Michael, want to come and play baseball with us after school?" Davey asked one day.

"Sure," said Michael. "You might have to help me a little, though."

"No problem!" exclaimed Davey.

At that very moment, somewhere up in Laughterland, Giggleina smiled, very proud of herself for helping someone share his gift of laughter.

As she looked down on them that night, she saw a little smile on Davey's face as he dreamed about how good it felt to make someone else happy. And, she saw a smile on Michael's face as he dreamed about his new friends.

She was already on the lookout for other little boys and girls that she could help to share their gifts of laughter. Is there someone you might like Giggleina to visit tonight?

About the Author

Pat hails from Bethlehem, Pennsylvania but has lived in NC since 1990. She is a wife, mother of four, and grandmother of five. A Registered Nurse, Pat graduated from St. Luke's Hospital School of Nursing in Bethlehem and has worked in several different areas of nursing during her career. Besides writing, Pat's first love is her family. She also enjoys sewing, gardening, and singing.

About the Illustrator

Lisa Lowell, originally from Orlando, Florida, is a wife and mother of five daughters. She has been creating murals for over 20 years and also works in the field of Histology. As she continues to create in many aspects of her life, her husband and daughters are treasuring memories as they grow older. Lisa is especially fulfilled when she is supporting those who need comfort.